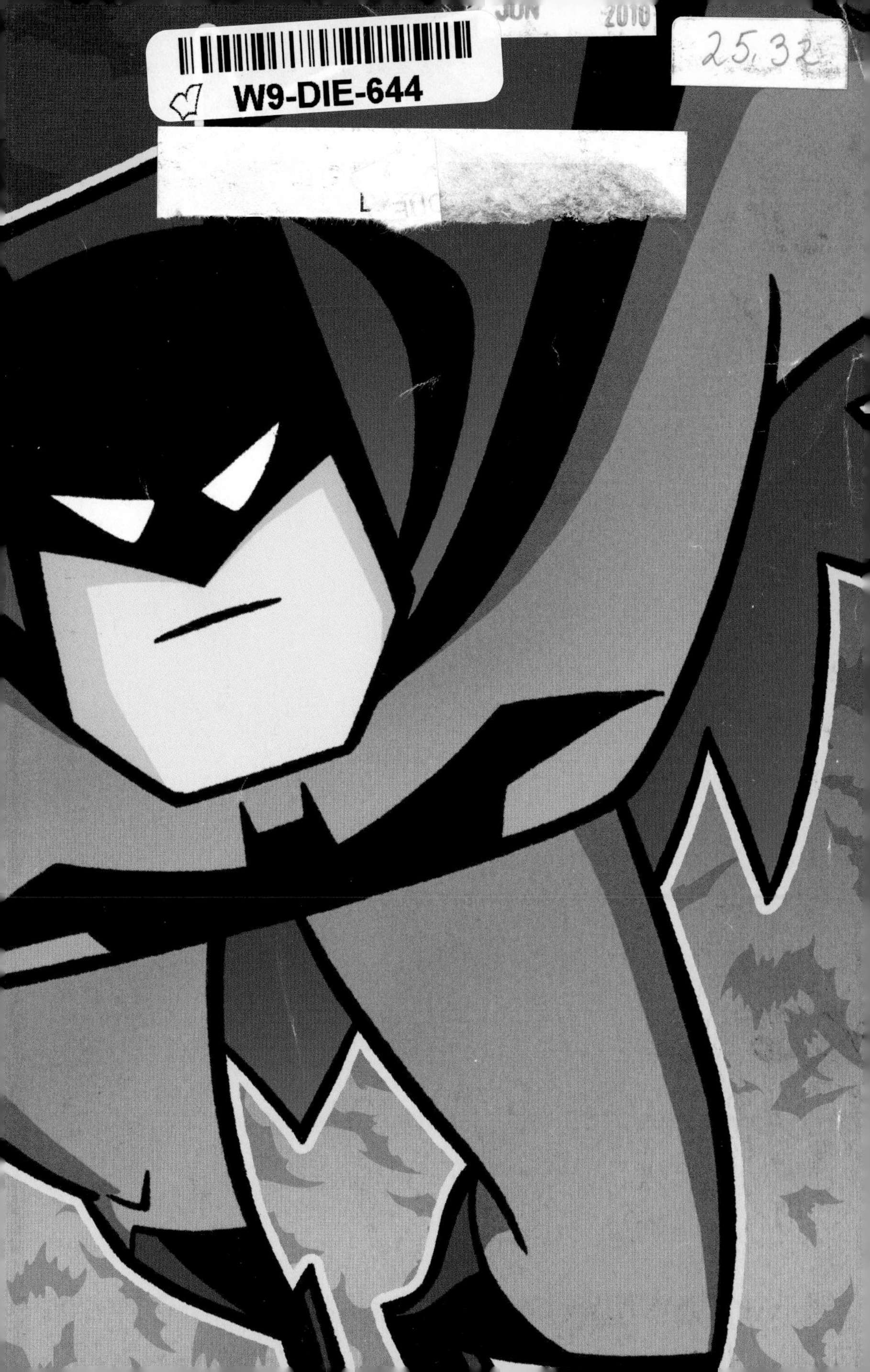

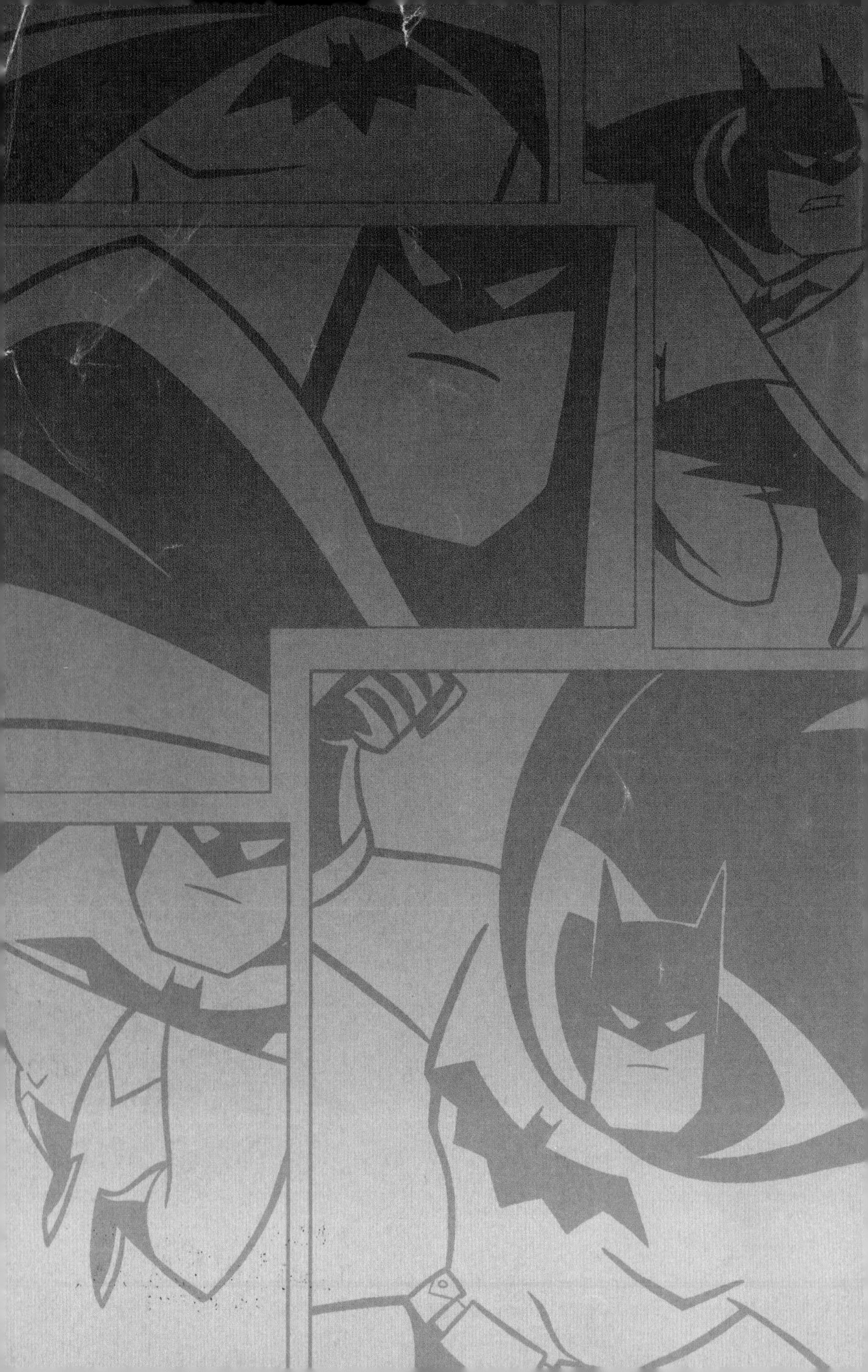

SUPER DC HEROES

BATMAN

THE MAN BEHIND THE MASK

WRITTEN BY
MICHAEL DAHL

ILLUSTRATED BY
DAN SCHOENING

BATMAN CREATED BY
BOB KANE

STONE ARCH BOOKS
MINNEAPOLIS   SAN DIEGO

...ished by Stone Arch Books in 2010,
A Capstone Imprint
... Good Counsel Drive, P.O. Box 669
Mankato, Minnesota 56002
www.capstonepub.com

Library of Congress Cataloging-in-Publication Data

Dahl, Michael.
  The man behind the mask / by Michael Dahl ; illustrated by Dan
Schoening.
    p. cm. -- (DC super heroes. Batman)
  ISBN 978-1-4342-1563-5 (lib. bdg.) -- ISBN 978-1-4342-1730-1 (pbk.)
[1. Superheroes--Fiction.] I. Schoening, Dan, ill. II. Title.
  PZ7.D15134Man 2010
  [Fic]--dc22

                        2009006303

Summary: Many years after the death of his parents, Bruce Wayne comes
face to face with their murderer, Joe Chill. While chasing down this
cold-blooded crook, Bruce recalls the story of his own past and the
evolution of his alter ego . . . Batman.

Art Director: Bob Lentz
Designer: Bob Lentz

Printed in the United States of America in Stevens Point, Wisconsin.
032010
005721R

TABLE of CONTENTS

CHAPTER 1

THE FACE IN THE SHADOWS

It was long past midnight in Gotham City. Most of the streets were empty. Old newspapers fluttered through damp alleys. Deep shadows hid under bridges. A lone armored truck drove down a side street on its way to a bank.

An explosive device, hidden in the street, blasted the truck. The vehicle was thrown on its side. It slid across the street and smashed into an empty parked car.

The driver and the security guards inside were tossed around like socks in a dryer. Car alarms filled the air. Flames shot up from the armored truck's engine.

"Help!" yelled a security guard. He pounded on the truck's rear door, which had been smashed shut. He couldn't call for help because his phone was ripped off its holder by the crash.

"We've got to get out of here!" the injured driver yelled. "In a few more seconds that engine is going to blow!"

Suddenly, two men leaped out of the shadows. They rushed over to the truck. They used a metal bar to force open the crushed truck door.

"Thanks," said one of the guards as he stumbled onto the street.

"Don't thank us yet," one of the strangers replied. He aimed a deadly weapon at the man. "Hand over your guns. Then hand over the cash, or your buddies stay inside the truck!"

Several moments later, the crooks were running down a dark alley, their backpacks stuffed with cash. The guards quickly helped each other out of the burning truck.

The armored truck exploded in a shower of glass and flame. The men were knocked off their feet and thrown against the rough surface of the street. The driver looked up just as a strange shape appeared in the smoke of the burning truck.

"What's that?" he yelled, pointing at the shape in the sky.

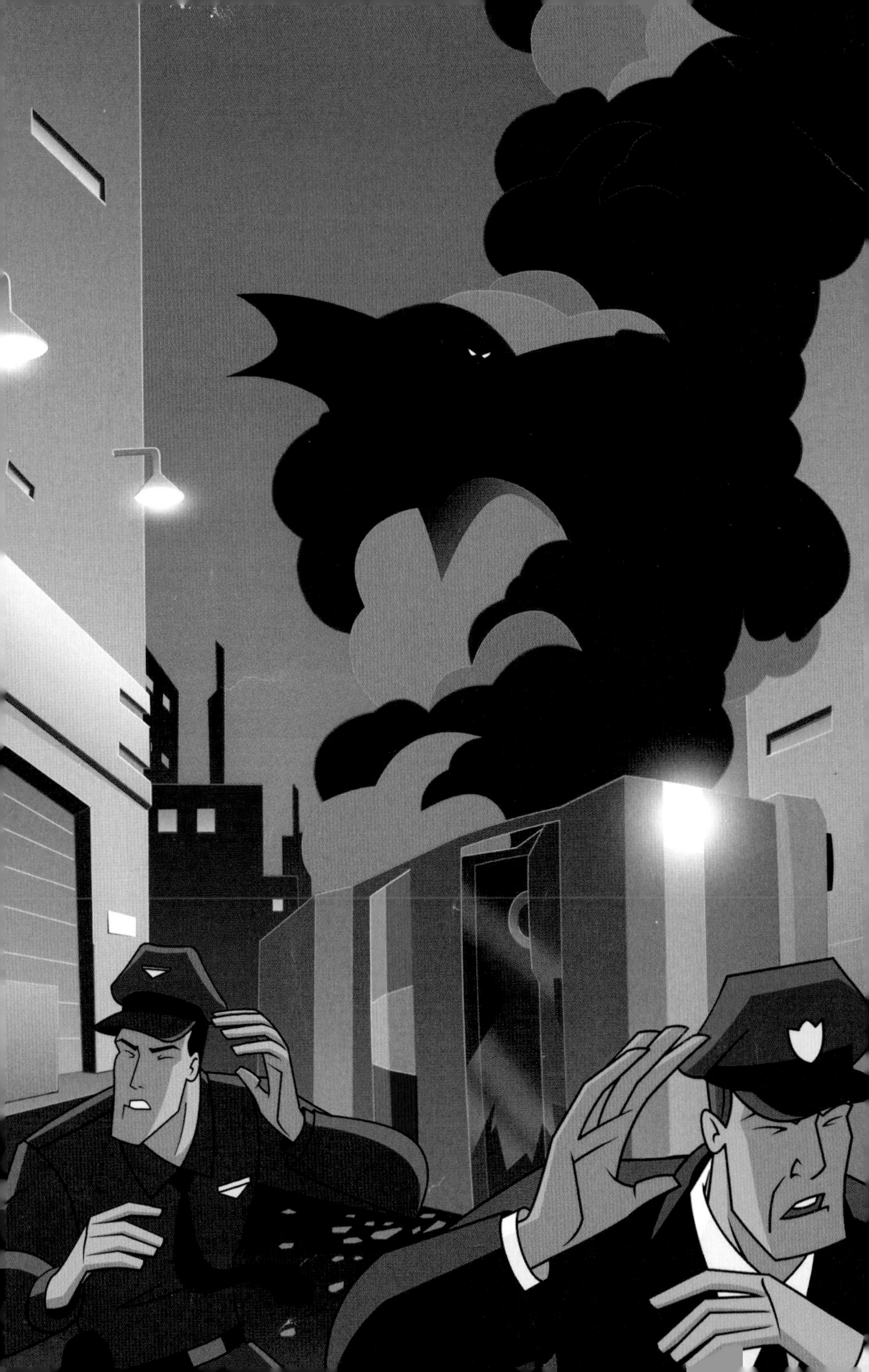

A bat-like figure swooped through the smoke and flames. He landed on the street without a sound.

"Batman!" cried one of the guards.

Gotham City's greatest hero glanced quickly at the men lying in the street. "Do you need help?" asked the Dark Knight.

"We're okay," the driver replied. "But the crooks are getting away!"

Another guard pointed down the alley. "They went down there," he alerted Batman.

Without a word, Batman turned and raced down the alley. His boots hardly made a sound against the pavement.

As he ran, he pressed a hidden button on the armored hood that protected his head. Night-vision lenses clicked on.

They allowed him to see clearly in the thickest shadows. They also showed him heat tracks left behind by warm bodies. Dozens of tiny paw prints made by rats covered the ground. Batman spied two trails of human shoe prints leading to the right, into another alley.

Suddenly, he heard men's voices. One of the voices sounded familiar. It was a voice he hadn't heard in years, but he couldn't match it to a face.

"You said we'd split the money," argued a voice. "I was the one who put that bomb in the street. I deserve more for taking that risk."

"Yeah, but it was my idea," said the familiar voice. "I was the one who did all the planning. Without my brains, you'd still be holding up drugstores."

Batman now saw the two men standing in a corner of the alley. They were two ordinary crooks wearing long coats and backpacks. One of the men had grabbed the other by the collar.

"Let me go!" the crook shouted.

Batman took a step forward. "You guys are just too greedy for your own good," he said. The crooks looked at him and gasped.

Batman turned off his night-vision lenses. Then he, too, took a deep breath.

The Caped Crusader was not often surprised, but as he stared at the men, he recognized one of them. The face was older, harder, and meaner, but it was a face he would never forget. The man's name was Joe Chill. Twenty years ago, he had killed Batman's parents.

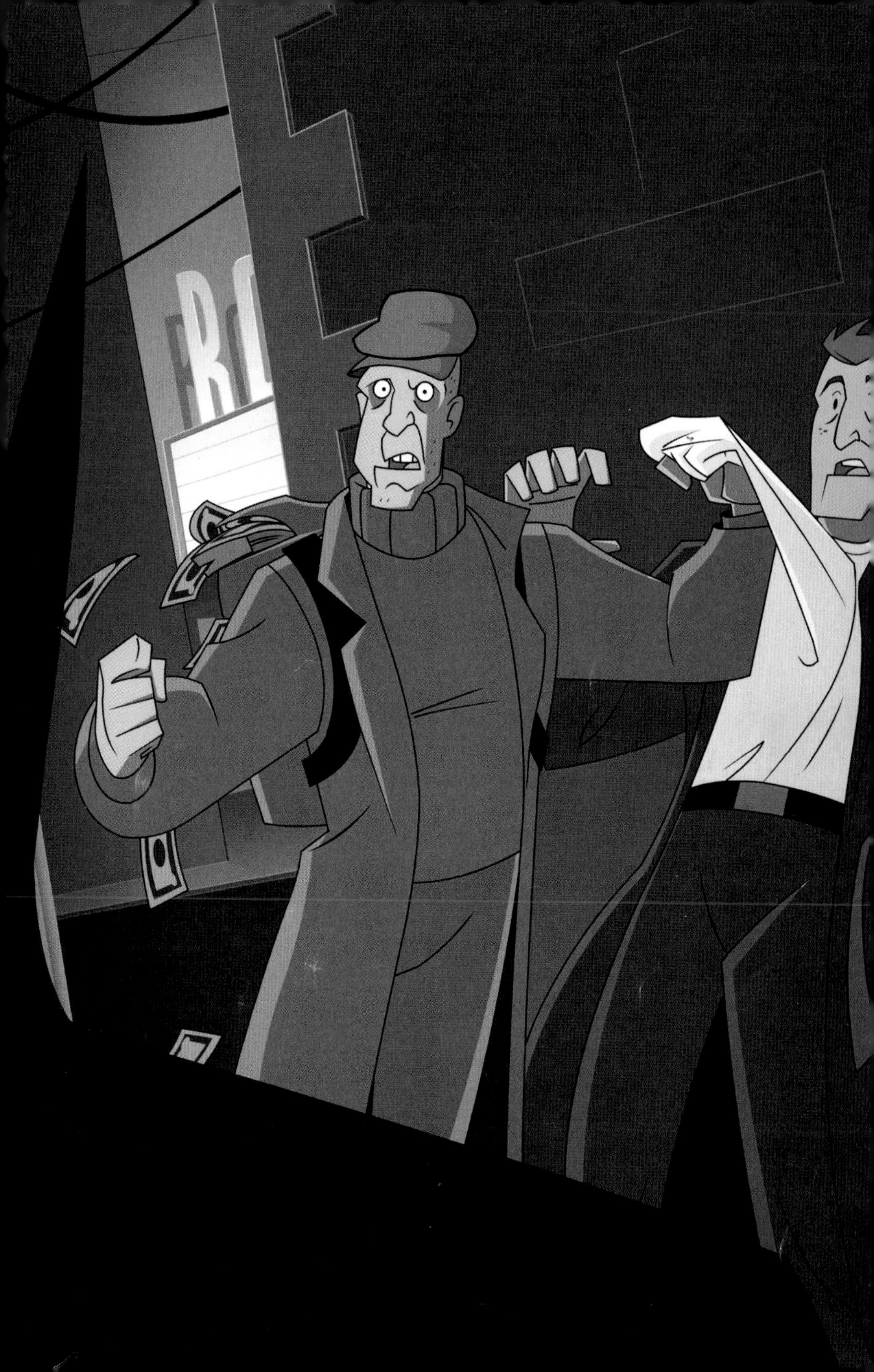

CHAPTER 2

THE MAN IN THE ALLEY

As Batman stared into Joe Chill's face, he remembered another night, a night that was dark and cold like this one. It was twenty years ago, when he was just a boy, before he became the man known as Batman. Then he was known by the name his parents had given him, Bruce Wayne.

"Bruce! Over here," yelled his father, Thomas Wayne. "Let's get some ice cream."

"Lovely," said his mother, Martha. "A dish of ice cream would be perfect. That movie house was so hot and stuffy."

"I didn't think it was too stuffy," said ten-year-old Bruce.

The family was just walking away from a movie theater. The cool night air was a welcome relief from the hot, blazing lights of the theater lobby.

"I'm sure you didn't," said Bruce's mother. "All you could think about was watching your hero on the screen."

"Zorro!" agreed Bruce. The boy leaped ahead of his parents and slashed a "Z" in the air with an imaginary sword. Then he turned around and looked up at his dad. "Can we come back tomorrow and see the *Mark of Zorro* again?" he asked.

Martha Wayne laughed. "Haven't you had enough of Zorro for one week?" she asked Bruce.

"He's the greatest hero in the world," said Bruce. "He always fights for justice. Never for rewards or fame. People don't know his secret identity, so they couldn't reward him even if they wanted to. I could see that movie a hundred times!"

"I admit, he is admirable," said Thomas Wayne.

"I want to be just like Zorro," said Bruce. "I'll wear a mask, and a long dark cape, and I'll —"

"Do you think Zorro likes ice cream?" asked his mother.

"Of course, he does," said Bruce. "His favorite is chocolate."

Now it was his father's turn to laugh. "Did they have ice cream back in Zorro's time?" asked Thomas Wayne.

"Sure they did, Dad," said Bruce. "The Persians invented ice cream thousands of years ago."

The Waynes were so busy laughing and talking that they hadn't been paying close attention to their surroundings. Thomas Wayne had led them down an alley behind the theater. He remembered seeing an all-night diner somewhere in that direction. It had a sign in the window advertising fifteen different flavors of ice cream. The diner was next to a subway stop, so it wouldn't be out of their way.

The alley was dark and cold. Old newspapers fluttered across the ground. Shadows crouched in the corners. Strange voices whispered through the darkness.

"Are you sure this is the way?" Martha asked her husband.

Bruce's ears pricked up at a strange sound. "Was that a bat?" he asked. Bruce was afraid of bats.

"No, kid. It was me." A stranger stepped out from behind a corner. He wore a shabby suit and a battered hat. He carried a gun in his right hand.

"Thomas!" whispered Martha.

"Stay calm," said Thomas Wayne. "Bruce, stand over there."

Bruce backed up from the crook. He bumped up against his mother and then stood there, frozen.

"Please, don't shoot," said Martha.

"I'm not planning on it, lady," said the man. "As long as your husband here hands over his wallet."

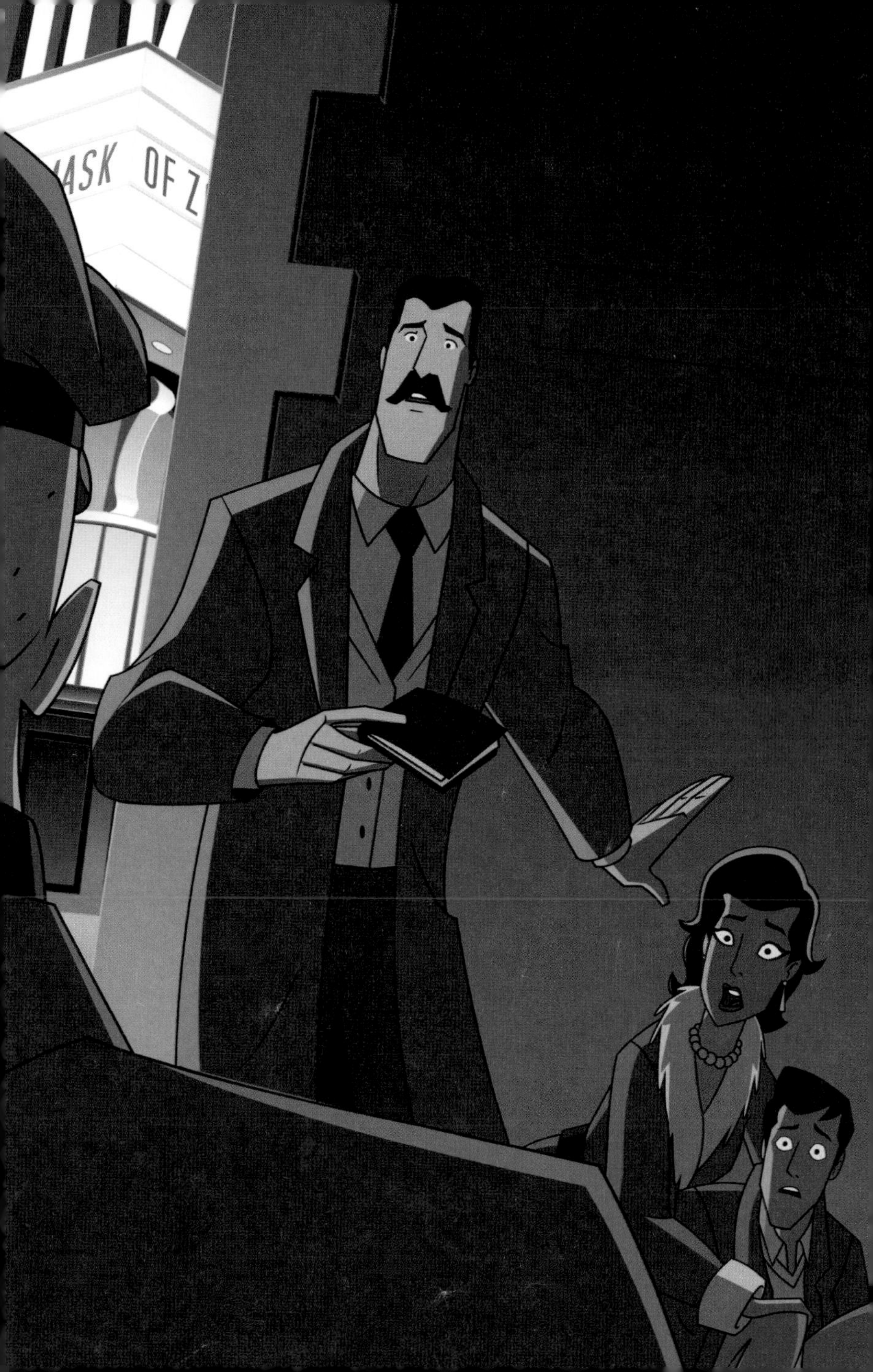
MASK OF Z

Martha was shivering.

"My wife has a fear of guns," said Thomas Wayne, quietly.

"I don't blame her," said the man. "Guns can be dangerous."

"Then why don't you just put that thing away," said Thomas, "and I'll give you whatever you want."

"Don't be a wiseguy, mister," said the man. "I'll put it away as soon as you hand over the cash."

The thief waved the weapon in Thomas Wayne's face. Thomas remained quiet, his breathing calm. Bruce could see his father moving slowly toward the crook.

"Please," said Martha, her voice rising in fear.

Thomas Wayne slowly reached into the pocket of his suit jacket. "All right, all right, let's just stay calm," he said.

"What are you doing?" asked the crook, nervously.

"I'm just reaching for my wallet," said Thomas.

"Guys carry their wallets in their back pockets," said the crook.

"Dad carries his wallet in his jacket," said Bruce.

"Oh, he does, does he?" asked the crook. He leaned down and stared menacingly into Bruce's pale face.

"Oh, Thomas," said Martha. "Help!"

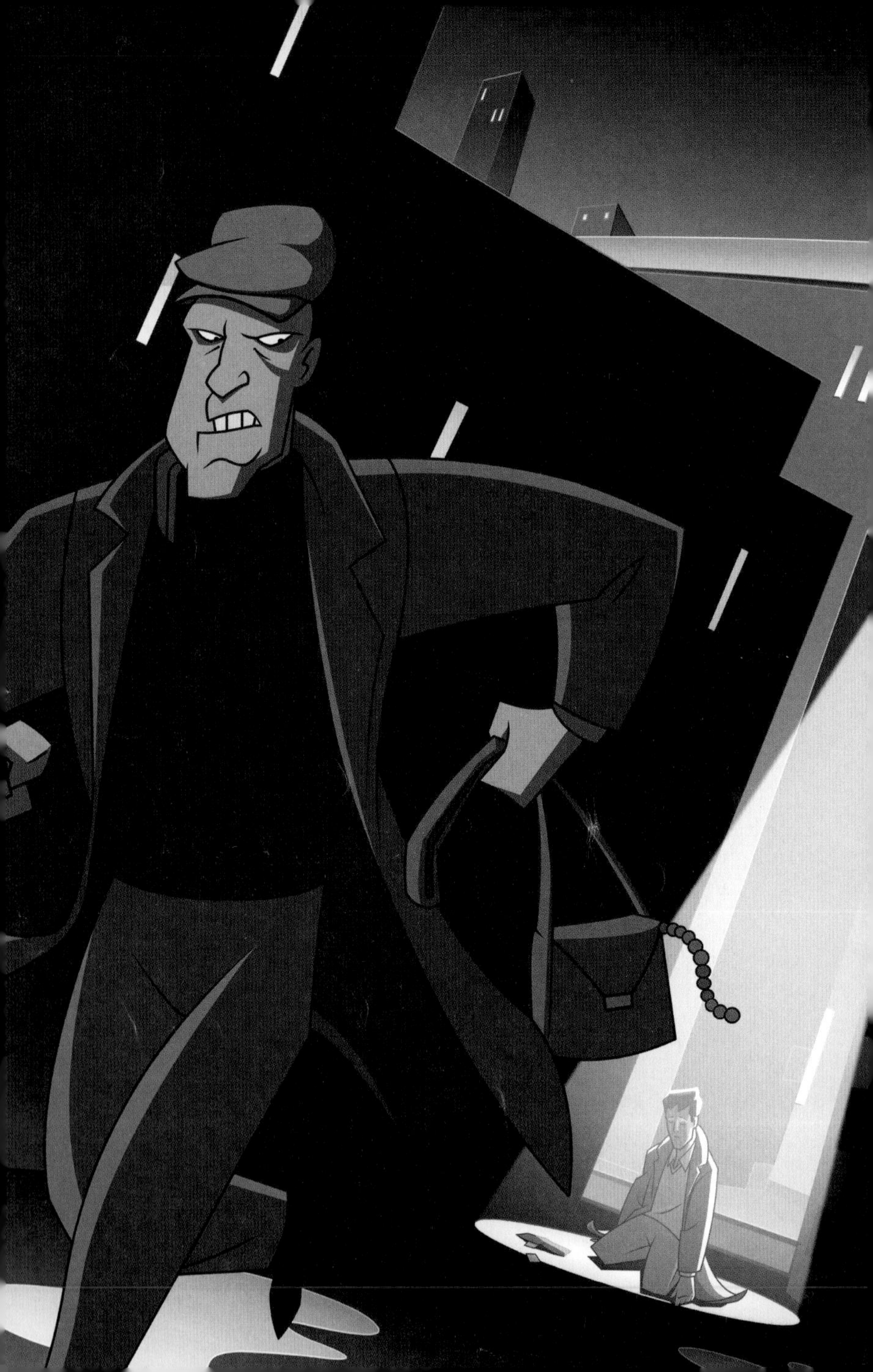

Bruce felt a cold rush of air behind him. He turned and looked. His father was lying in the alley.

"Help! Someone help!" he heard his mother cry.

The crook was leaning over Bruce's father, tugging at the wallet in his hand. Then he ran away. His footsteps pounded on the wet floor of the alley. The darkness seemed to swirl around Bruce and swallow him up.

But now, twenty years later, the same thief was standing there. Joe Chill. He was not running away now.

Mom and Dad, thought Bruce Wayne, now disguised as Batman. *I can finally bring you justice.*

Joe Chill suddenly reached into his backpack and pulled out a smoke bomb.

The alley flooded with thick, black clouds.

CHAPTER 3

BIRTH OF A CRIME FIGHTER

Batman's sharp ears heard the quiet click of a weapon. The crime fighter quickly jumped out of the way.

POP! Somewhere, hidden in the thick smoke, one of the crooks had tried shooting him. Luckily, Batman's quick reflexes saved him as he swiftly dived to safety.

He pulled a gas mask out of his Utility Belt and attached it to his hood. Now he could breathe safely. If the smoke bomb were poisonous, the mask would filter out any dangerous chemicals.

"Uhhh!" Batman heard a groan.

The Dark Knight rushed forward and stepped out of the smoke cloud. Joe Chill was gone. His partner was lying on the ground, grabbing his shoulder in pain.

"I can't believe it," croaked the thief. "His own partner. He shot his own partner."

"Joe Chill is ruthless," Batman growled in a low voice.

The thief's eyes opened wide. "You know him?" he asked.

"More than you know," said Batman. He put the gas mask back into his belt as the air cleared.

The wounded thief glanced around. "Hey! He stole my backpack!" he cried. "Chill took all the loot!"

A grim smile appeared on Batman's face. "He won't get far," he whispered.

Sirens filled the air. At the other end of the alley, police officers and squad cars appeared, circling the burning armored truck. Batman pressed a button on his belt. He spoke a few words into a hidden microphone built into his hood. There was a crackling sound and then a voice. His microphone had radioed the police.

"I have one of the criminals here in the alley," said Batman. "He needs medical assistance."

"We're on our way, Batman," an officer replied.

"Jeez, it really hurts," said the thief, still holding his shoulder. "Can you make them hurry?"

The Caped Crusader stared down at the injured crook. He saw the blood on the crook's hand and on the sleeve of his coat.

"I hate guns," said Batman.

Swiftly, the hero turned and began to rush after the escaping criminal.

"Batman!" the crook yelled. "Chill was supposed to have a motorcycle stashed a block away from here in Crime Alley — for our getaway. Of course, now I don't know if I believe anything he said."

Batman nodded, and then he turned his night-vision lenses back on. Red, glowing footprints appeared in front of him, leading him down the alley.

Now that he knew Joe Chill was armed, Batman was more cautious. He stayed in the shadows as he chased his prey.

Special antennas in his hood's ears helped him pick up the slightest sound. He tried to ignore the normal sounds of the night. He paid no attention to taxis several blocks away. He didn't listen to stray dogs snuffling through garbage. Instead, he listened only for the faint patter of running feet. He also listened for the click of a key fitting into a motorcycle's ignition switch.

After a few minutes of running, Batman had a strange feeling. He glanced quickly to his left and saw the roof of a familiar building — the old movie theater. The theater's lights had long since been shut off. The building had been closed for many years, but Batman could never forget this place. He and his parents had walked through this alley to find the diner that served ice cream.

In the alley, Batman's life had changed forever. Years later, Bruce had found out that the police called the place Crime Alley. It had certainly earned its deadly nickname.

After his parents' deaths, Bruce had dedicated his life to fighting crime. He didn't want anyone else to feel the pain that he had felt as a young boy. The pain of losing those he loved the most. His father had been a doctor and had spent his life healing people, saving their lives. Now, the same spirit lived on in his son.

Bruce spent years building up his body. He knew that fighting crime would require him to be in perfect physical shape. He learned gymnastics and swimming and boxing. He learned martial arts from ninja warriors.

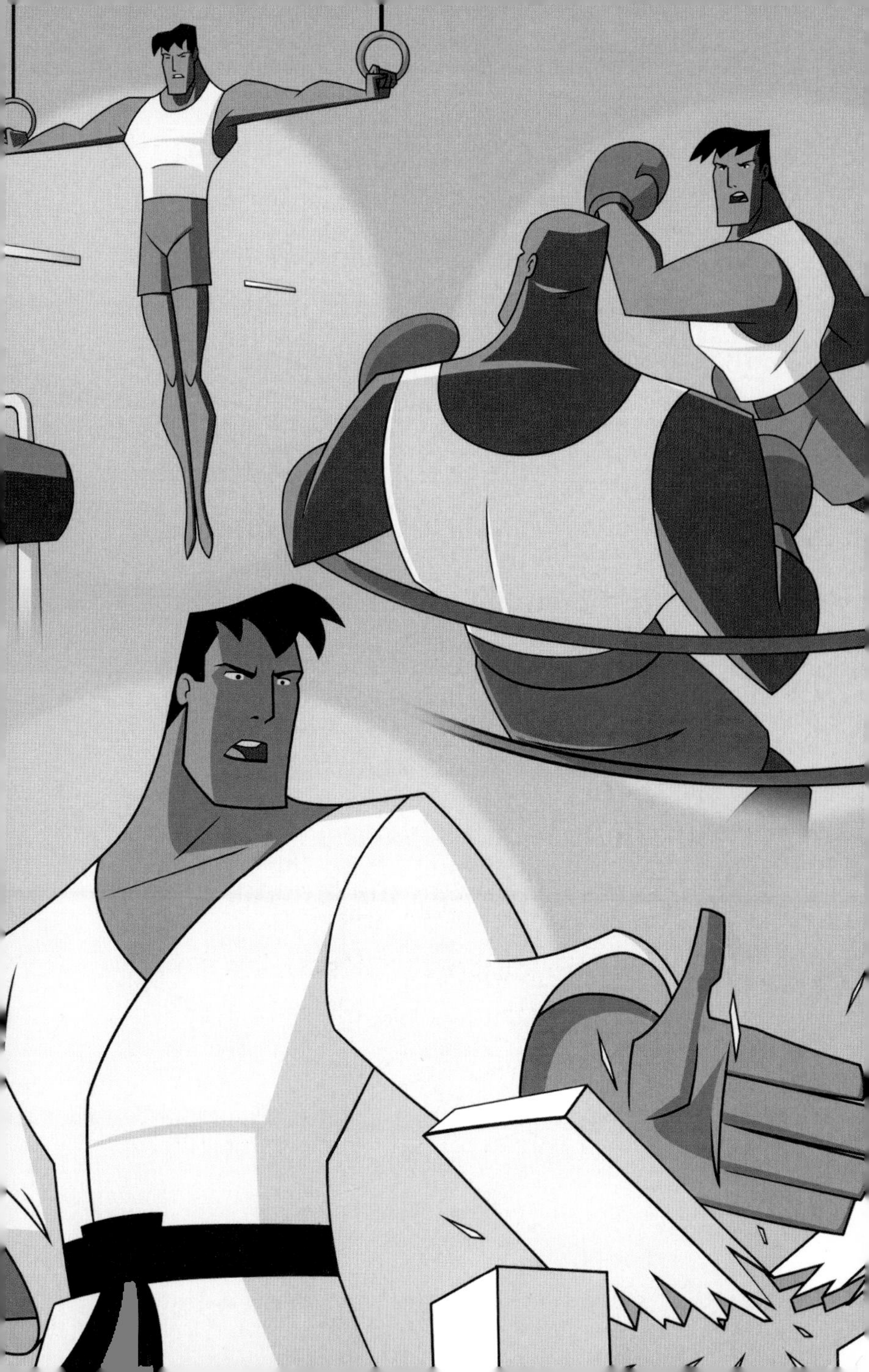

He had also been taught by African hunters how to track criminals. He needed all his skills to find his special prey.

CRASH!! A garbage can tipped over and rolled across Batman's path, bringing him back to the present. *Was that from a dog, or from Joe Chill?* he wondered.

Another metallic sound ripped through the night air.

SKREEEEEEECH!

Batman turned his head. A set of fire escape stairs fell toward the ground.

CHAPTER 4

BATARANG!

As Batman turned to face the falling metal stairs, his sharp hearing picked up another sound. He heard a man breathing behind him. Batman ducked just in time!

ZING! A bullet bounced off the brick wall near his head.

Joe Chill was hiding in the shadows. He had used the falling fire escape stairs to distract the Dark Knight. But his plan didn't work.

Quickly, Batman jumped to his feet.

VROOOOOM!

A motorcycle engine roared to life. Batman saw Joe Chill race down the alley on the back of a sports bike.

Chill looked back and fired again. He knew it would be almost impossible to hit his target while moving on a bike. Instead, he was hoping to slow Batman down. But the Caped Crusader easily dodged out of the way of the bullet.

Batman hated guns. He had vowed never to use one since that was how his parents had been killed. Instead, he used other weapons. Right now he had only seconds before Chill's bike got too far away. He reached into his belt and pulled out a Batarang. With a movement he had practiced over and over, Batman flipped the metal object at the bike.

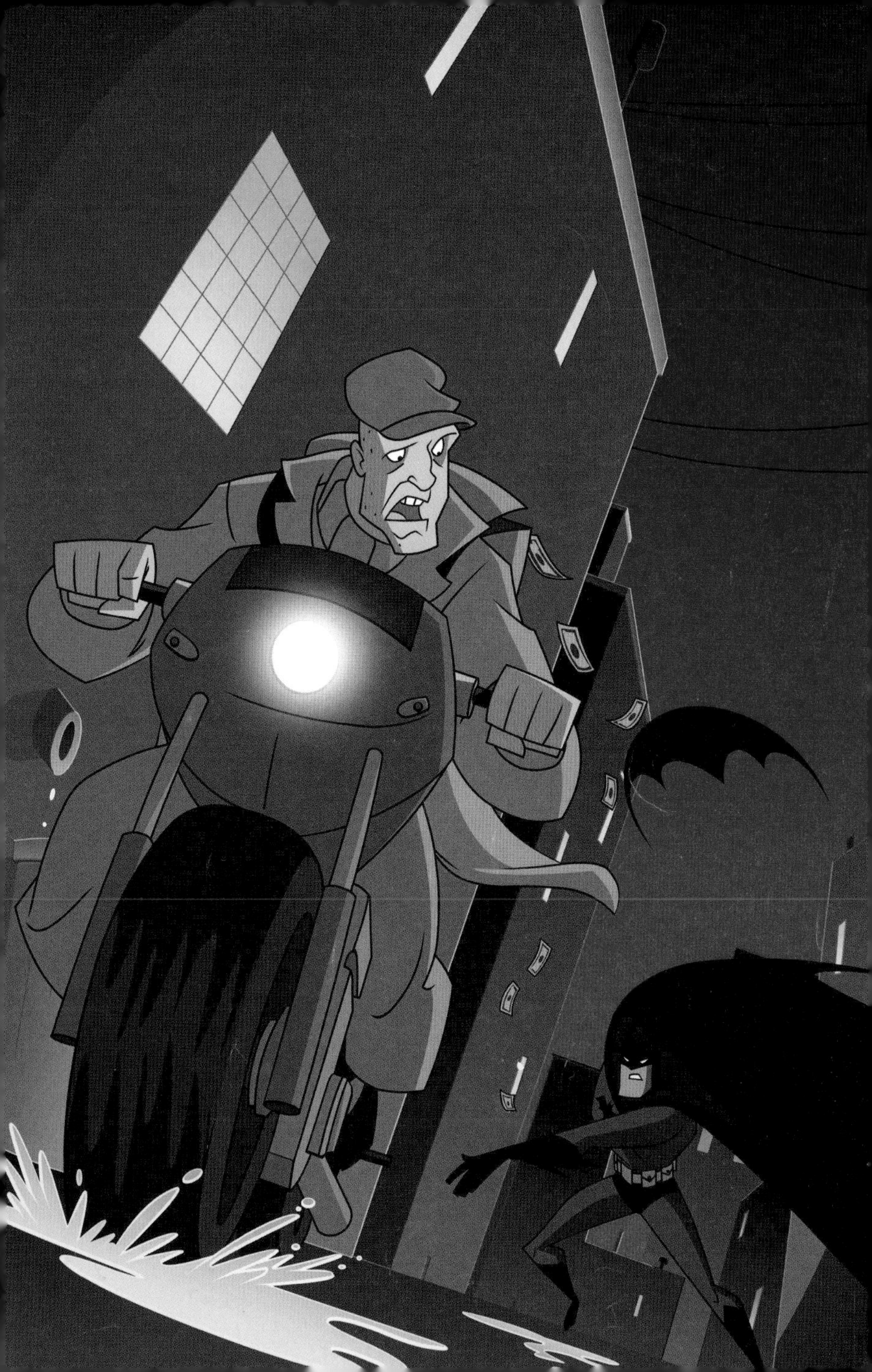

Years ago, Batman had made these small weapons in his special lab, the Batcave. In that secret hideaway, deep beneath his home, Wayne Manor, Batman had created dozens of amazing devices. Each one would help him in his fight against crime.

Now, the small bat-like weapon zipped through the air. It flew like a rocket down the alley. Before Joe Chill could gun his bike's engine, the tip of the Batarang sliced into the rear tire.

"No!" Chill yelled.

SKREEE-EEE-EEECH!

The motorcycle tire ripped apart. The bike flew out of control. It slammed against the alley wall and threw Joe Chill farther down the alley.

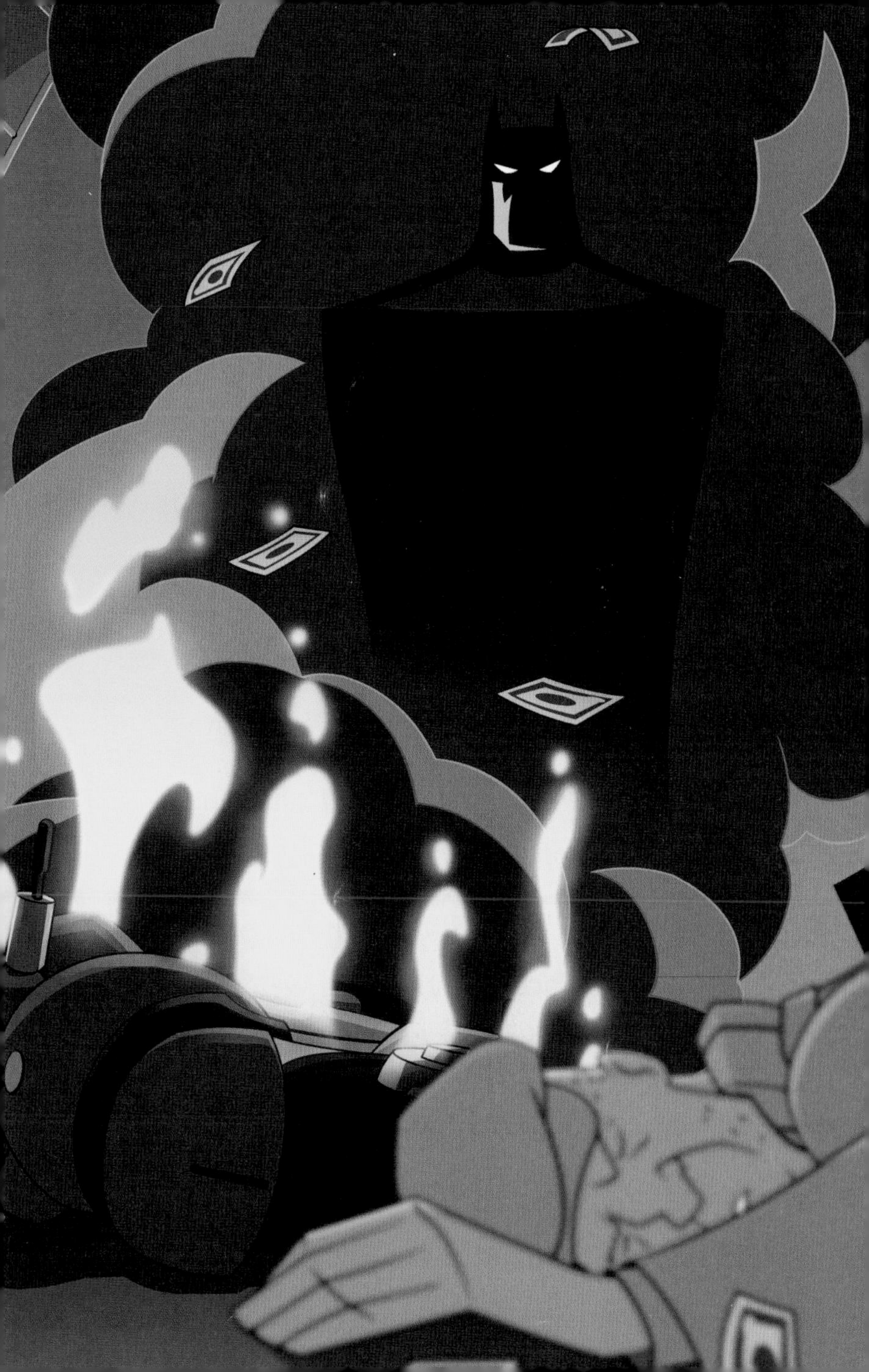

His face was cut and his hands were scraped, but the crook would not give up. He'd planned too hard, and waited too long to make this much money in a single night. He crawled to his feet, grabbed his backpacks, and ran down the street.

Behind him, Batman stopped for only a few seconds at the wrecked motorcycle. Lying on the ground, near the rear tire of the bike, Batman saw a metal object. It was not the Batarang. It was Joe Chill's gun.

Perfect, thought Batman. *It's just the evidence the police need to put Chill away.*

Too often, crooks did not go to prison because of a lack of evidence. When Batman was training, he studied forensics, the science of investigating crimes. He knew that evidence was a key factor in proving the case against a crook like Chill.

Batman stared at the gun's handle through his night-vision lenses. He saw four red glowing marks. Perfect finger prints. Police scientists would be able to match these with Chill's prints taken from him the last time he was arrested.

Investigators would also find the bullet casings from the three times Chill shot his gun during the night. Once at his partner, and twice when he missed Batman. It would be easy to convict Chill of armed robbery. There were plenty of witnesses from the armored truck that blew up. But now, with this gun evidence, Chill would also face the heavier penalty of assault with a deadly weapon.

Batman would tell the police later where to find the gun. Right now, he needed to catch Chill.

Batman looked up. He heard the sound of running. On foot, Joe Chill would not get far. Batman knew the dark streets and alleys of Gotham City better than anyone.

Batman also knew better than anyone that it was useless to outrun the law. And tonight he had an even stronger reason for tracking down his prey. This was the man who had robbed the Dark Knight of his family. This was the man who had taken away the two people Batman had loved most.

"This time," Batman said to himself, "Chill is not getting away."

CHAPTER 5

SHADOW OF THE BAT

Batman wondered how Chill could keep running. It must have been the fear in his muscles. Far ahead, Chill turned down another alley. Batman blamed himself for staying too long at the motorcycle. He should have caught Chill first and then come back to the bike.

Batman fired a grappling hook at a nearby building. The hook's wire pulled him up over the street. It was faster to soar above the streets than to travel by foot. Still, Joe Chill was almost a block away.

From his higher viewpoint, Batman noticed an unused spotlight near the alley. It sat in front of a closed-up store. The light must have been used for a special sale or grand opening. Batman pulled another Batarang from his belt. This one was smaller than the others. It was only used when Batman needed to hit a very small target. Tonight, his target was a button on the side of the spotlight.

Batman aimed and tossed.

The Batarang hit the button. The searchlight's beam shot down the alley. Shadows disappeared in a blast of white light. Then Batman slid down his wire. He dropped directly into the path of the beam of light.

At the other end of the alley, Chill came to a dead stop. "What?" he yelled. "It's not possible!"

A brick wall in front of him suddenly lit up from the searchlight. There on the wall, in the middle of the light, loomed the giant shadow of a bat.

"No! Get away from me!" Chill cried out in fear.

The shadow of a Batarang was being projected on the wall by the searchlight. It looked like a version of the Bat-Signal, used to summon Batman when the police needed him.

The bat shadow grew larger. Chill was not sure where to turn. He stepped back. Then he bumped up against a body behind him. Chill spun around and froze.

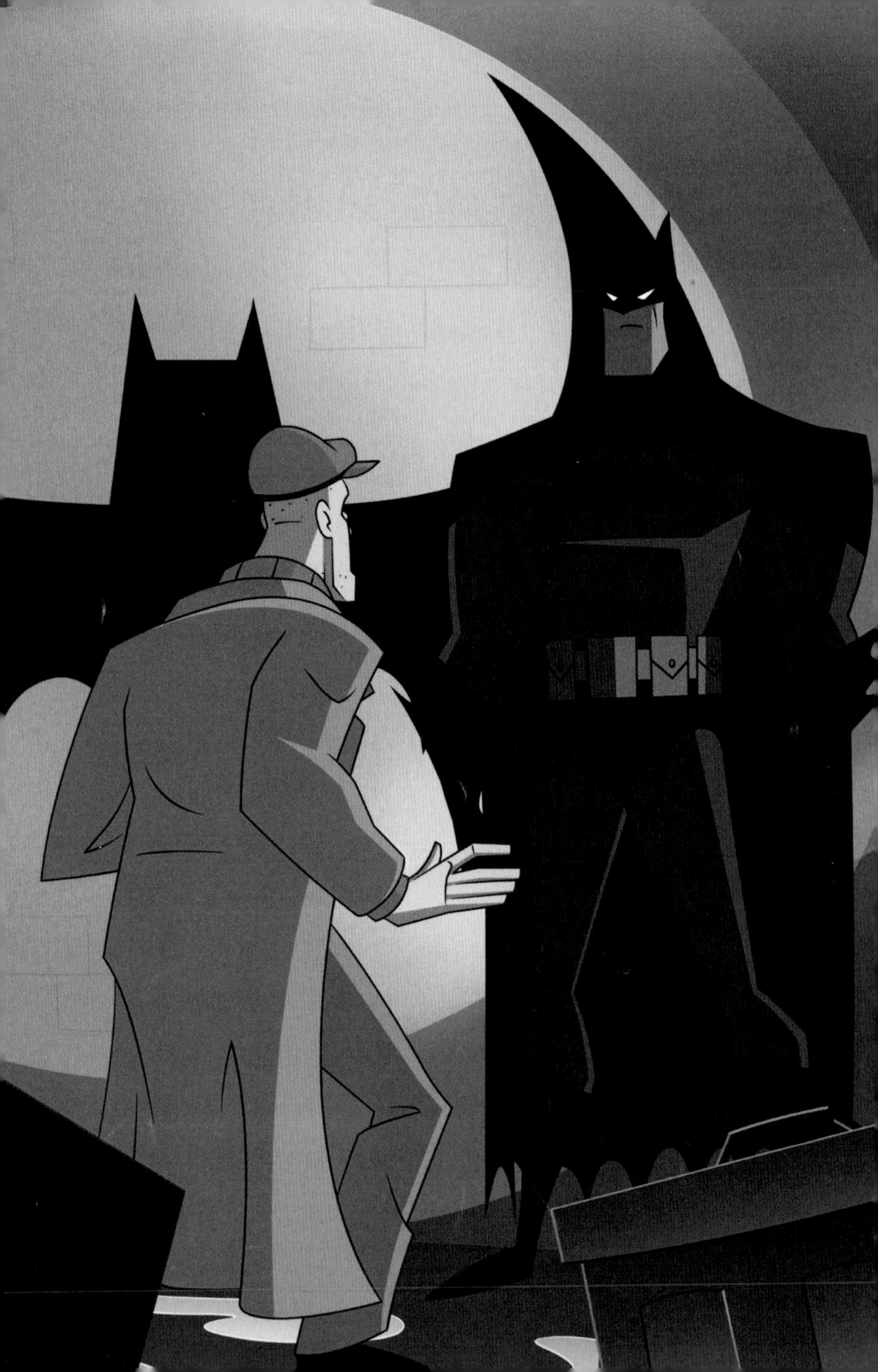

"But Batman," said Chill. "How did you get behind me? I thought that was you!"

Batman had pulled a thin, strong wire from his Utility Belt and began tying up Chill's hands. "Not afraid of a little bat, are you, Chill?" Batman asked, smiling.

The hero remembered another night, years ago, when he was alone and sitting in his house. Bruce Wayne was a grown man, ready to start his career as a crime fighter. He had trained and studied and practiced. All he needed then was a sign. In his heart he had asked his parents to send a signal that it was time to begin.

THUD! Bruce was startled by a bat flying into the window. That was the sign, Batman remembered. When he was a young boy, Bruce had been frightened by bats.

His mother and father had comforted him. They told him that bats were nothing to be afraid of. Now the grown-up Bruce wanted to put fear into the hearts of those who broke the law. He would use their fear against them. He would disguise himself as a giant bat — as a Batman.

Batman shot his grappling device toward the top of a nearby building. He held onto the wire using a special grip built into his armored gloves. *Zip!* Now it pulled him upward, along with his tied-up prey.

The Dark Knight soared back through the alleyways. From building to building, the wires pulled him along like a shadowy acrobat. He flew twenty, thirty feet above the ground. Joe Chill screamed in fright the whole way.

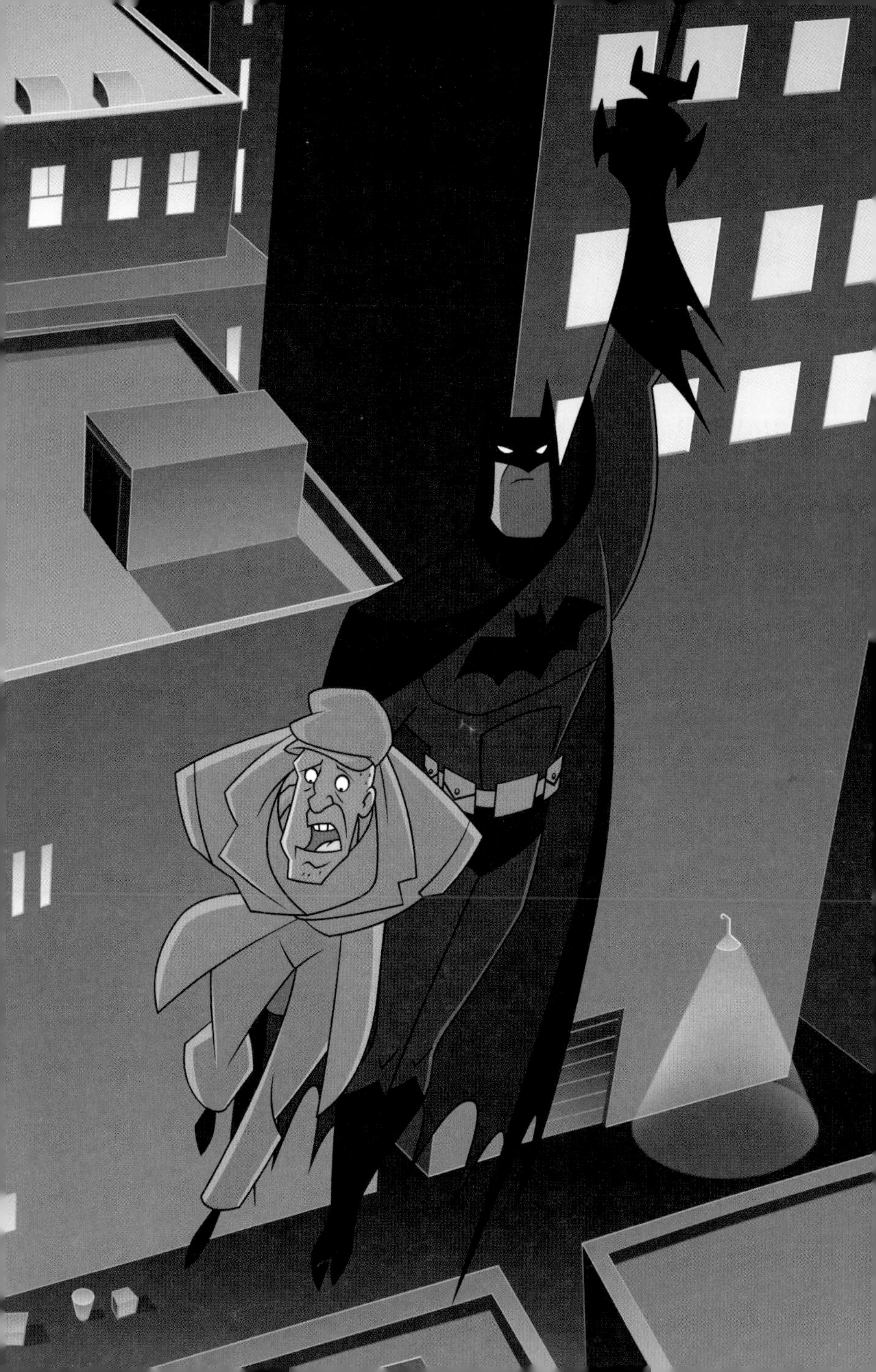

In a few minutes, the smell of burning metal filled the air. Batman had returned to the scene of the crime. Below him, he could see the armored truck. Its fire had been put out by a team of firefighters. Paramedics were now helping the injured security guards. Officers had the whole area blocked off with police tape. Reporters and TV cameras were filling the streets.

With a snap of his cape, Batman landed on the ground in front of a police squad car. He freed Joe Chill from the grappling wire and handed him over to one of the officers. He jerked his thumb over his shoulder. "You'll find some evidence about a hundred yards down that alley," he said.

Several reporters started to run toward him. They smelled a story. Batman knew it was time to go.

He looked up at a nearby clock. It had only been twenty minutes since he had left the burning truck to find and capture Joe Chill. Twenty minutes. To Batman, it had felt like twenty years.

"Thanks, Batman," yelled a police officer as the hero began to walk away. "So this is the guy who blew up the truck?"

Batman nodded.

"He looks sort of familiar," said an older officer.

"Nah," said his partner. "He's just another dumb criminal."

"I've never seen him before," said a reporter.

"He's a small-time crook," another reporter said. "No one important."

The officers and reporters would never know just how important the crook was. Just as they would never know it was Bruce Wayne's face behind the mask of the Dark Knight. A dark mask inspired by the one worn by his boyhood hero, Zorro.

"Hey, where did Batman go?" asked the reporter.

A shadow shaped like a bat flew silently overhead.

Rest in peace, Mom and Dad, thought Bruce as he quietly swooped off into the darkness. *Rest in peace.*

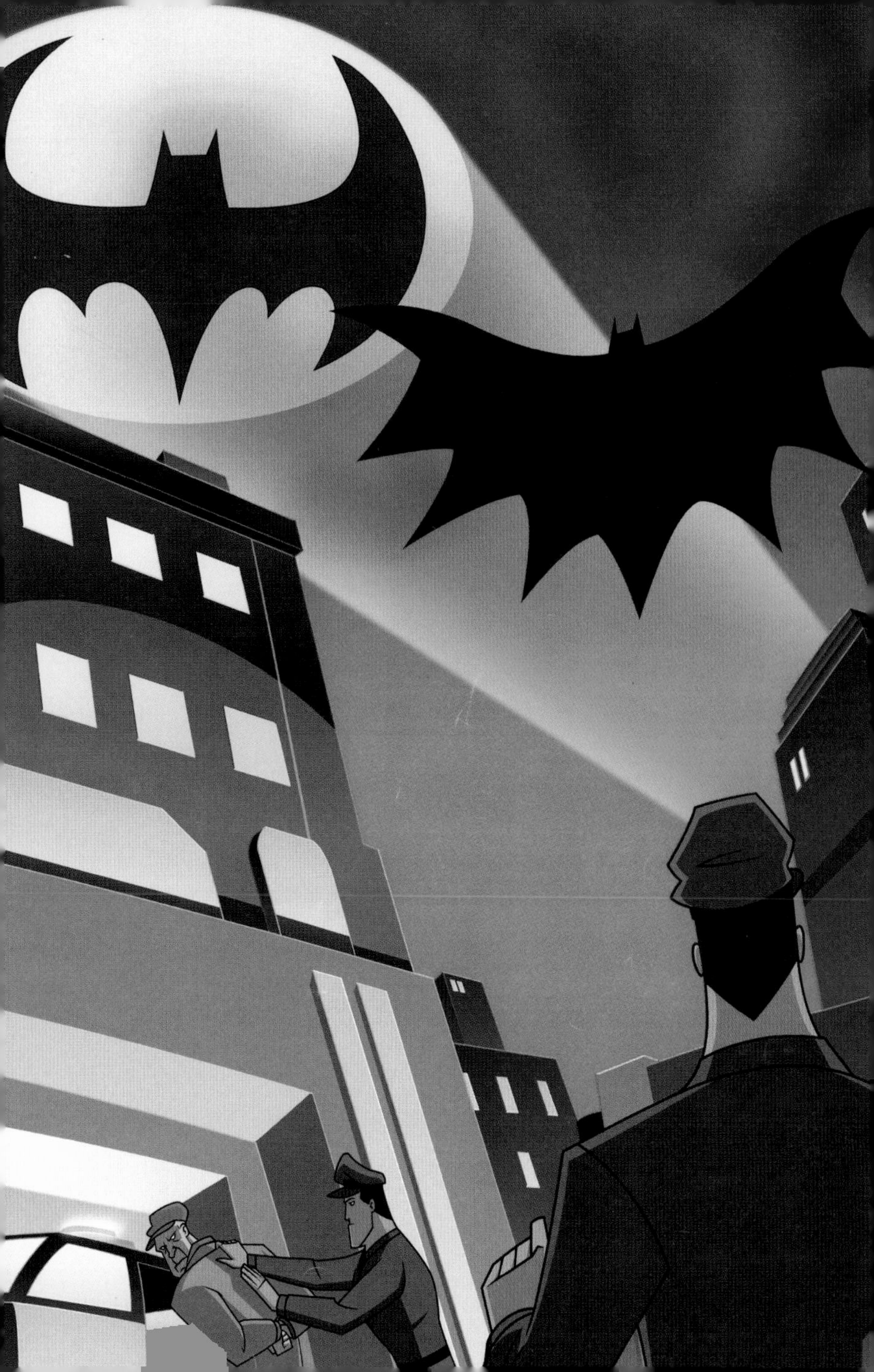

Wayne Murders, The

LEAD SUSPECT: Joe Chill

CRIME: Robbery, Murder

VICTIMS: Martha Wayne, Dr. Thomas Wayne

TIME OF OFFENSE:
6/26, 10:47 p.m.

LOCATION:
Crime Alley

CITY:
Gotham City

SURVIVING VICTIM:
Bruce Wayne, son

CASE SUMMARY:

The tragic slaying of Martha and Dr. Thomas Wayne occurred in Crime Alley on June 26 at 10:47 p.m. The Waynes were one of the wealthiest families in Gotham City. Sole witness to the crime is ten-year-old Bruce Wayne, son of Martha and Thomas. Life-long felon Joe Chill is the lead suspect and wanted for questioning. Chill's motive is unknown but evidence suggests that robbery was the main reason.

G.C.P.D. GOTHAM CITY POLICE DEPARTMENT

- Thomas Wayne was a gifted surgeon and philanthropist. He spent a large sum of money on charities and humanitarian efforts. As owner and president of Wayne Enterprises, Thomas's business efforts helped to revitalize Gotham. His son, Bruce, will eventually become president of Wayne Enterprises. However, Lucius Fox will run the company until Bruce comes of age.

- Martha Wayne was married to Thomas Wayne. Martha also came from a wealthy family. She supported various causes to help Gotham City regain its lost glory. In particular, Martha worked to protect and care for the orphans of Gotham City.

- Bruce Wayne, son of Thomas and Martha, survives as sole heir to the Wayne family fortune. A psychiatric evaluation suggests that Bruce has taken the death of his parents very hard. It should be noted that Bruce also has a severe fear of bats, stemming from a childhood incident in a cave.

- Alfred Pennyworth, the Wayne family butler, will raise the orphaned son, Bruce Wayne.

CONFIDENTIAL

BIOGRAPHIES

Michael Dahl is the author of more than 200 books for children and young adults. He has won the AEP Distinguished Achievement Award three times for his non-fiction books. His Finnegan Zwake mystery series was shortlisted twice by the Anthony and Agatha awards. Michael has also written the Library of Doom series and the Dragonblood books. He is a featured speaker at conferences around the country on graphic novels and high-interest books for boys.

Dan Schoening was born in Victoria, British Columbia, Canada. From an early age, Dan has had a passion for animation and comic books. Currently, Dan does freelance work in the animation and game industry and spends a lot of time with his lovely little daughter, Paige.

GLOSSARY

acrobat (AK-ruh-bat)—a person who performs gymnastic acts that require great skill

alerted (uh-LERT-id)—warned or pointed out something

cautious (KAW-shuhss)—if you are cautious, you try to avoid mistakes or danger

dedicated (DED-uh-kate-id)—focused heavily on something

evidence (EV-uh-duhnss)—information or items that help prove something

loomed (LOOMD)—appeared or hovered above in a sudden or frightening way

menacingly (MEN-uhss-ing-lee)—in a threatening or dangerous way

ruthless (ROOTH-liss)—cruel and without pity

Utility Belt (yoo-TIL-uh-tee BELT)—Batman's belt, which holds all of his weaponry and gadgets

DISCUSSION QUESTIONS

1. In this story, do you think Batman is more like a detective or more like a super hero? Why?

2. Batman didn't say who Joe Chill was when he handed him over to the police. Would you have told them? Why or why not?

WRITING PROMPTS

1. Joe Chill betrays his partner in crime. Have you ever been lied to? How did it make you feel? Did you forgive the person who lied? Write about it.

2. Before Bruce Wayne became Batman, he had a fear of bats. What kinds of things frighten you? What fears have you overcome as you've grown older?

3. Most graphic novels are written by one person and illustrated by someone else. Write a short story of your own, and then give it to a friend to illustrate.

WAIT!!

DON'T CLOSE THE BOOK!

THERE'S MORE!

FIND MORE:
GAMES & PUZZLES
HEROES & VILLAINS
AUTHORS & ILLUSTRATORS

AT...

www.CAPSTONEKIDS.com

STILL WANT MORE?
FIND COOL WEBSITES AND MORE BOOKS LIKE THIS ONE AT
WWW.FACTHOUND.COM. JUST TYPE IN THE BOOK ID:
1434215636 AND YOU'RE READY TO GO!

MORE NEW BATMAN ADVENTURES!

ARCTIC ATTACK

CATWOMAN'S
CLASSROOM OF CLAWS

HARLEY QUINN'S
SHOCKING SURPRISE

MY FROZEN VALENTINE

THE PUPPET MASTER'S
REVENGE

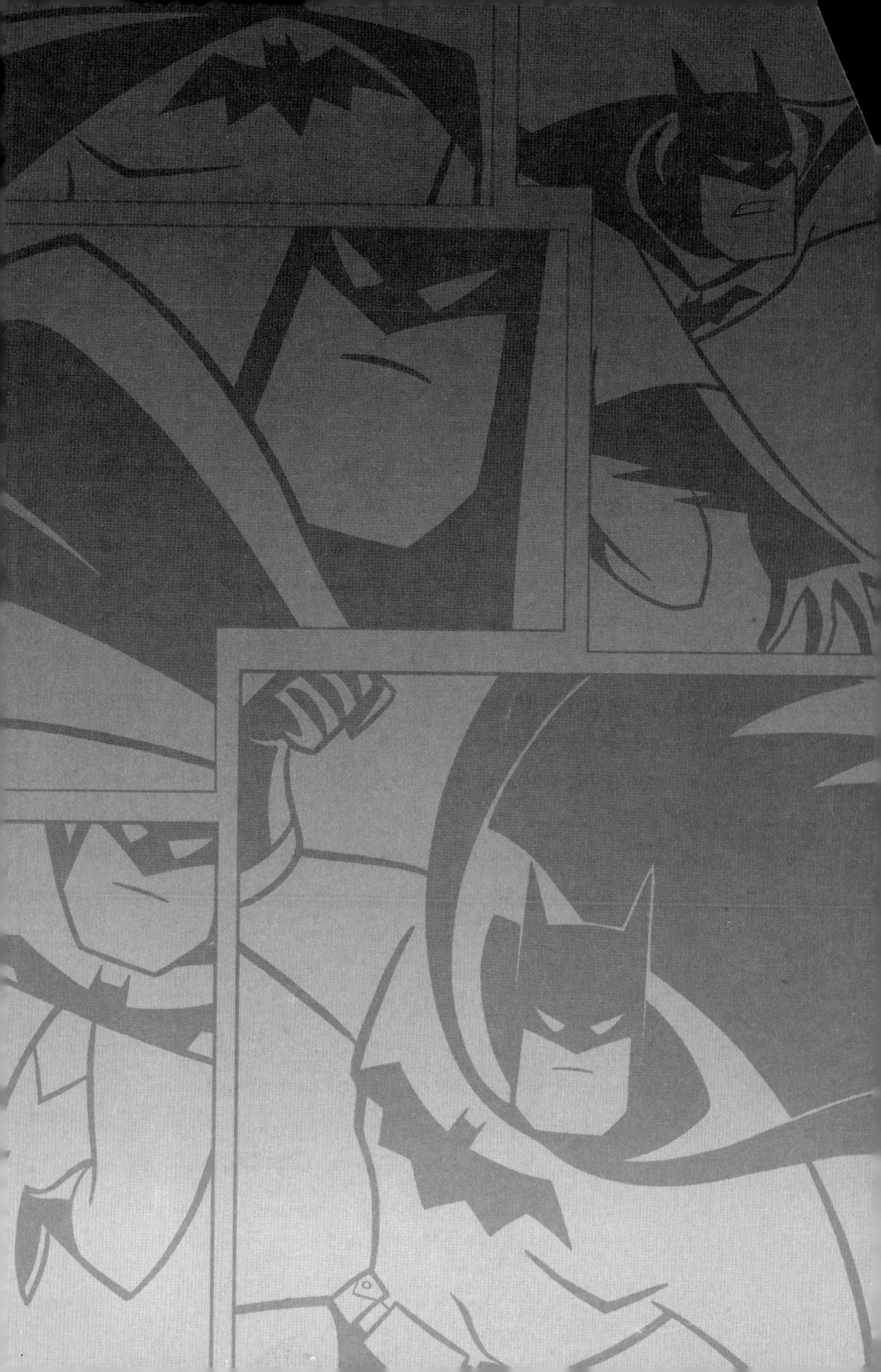

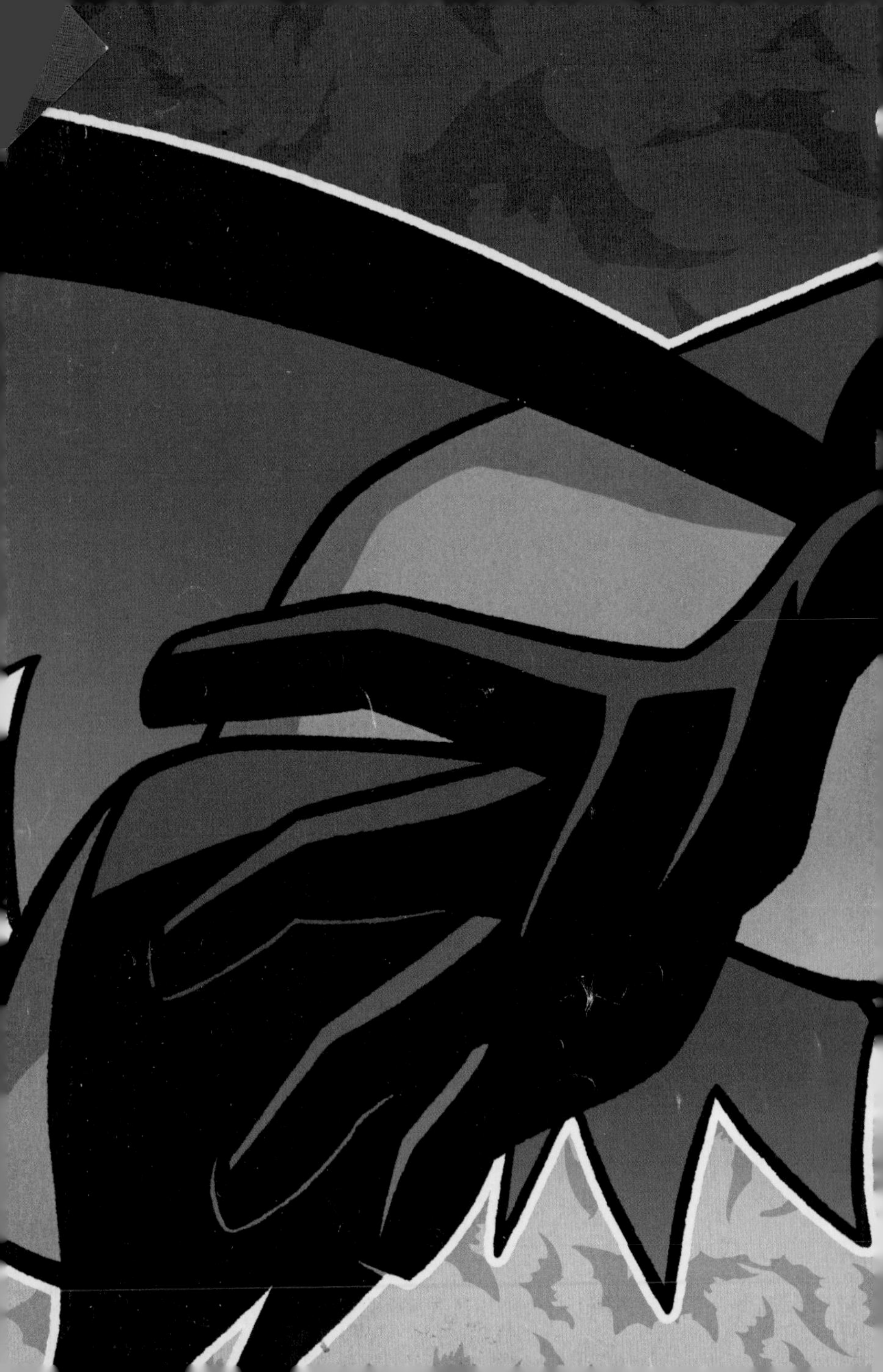